THE SNOOPY SHOW

NEST FRIENDS

by Charles M. Schulz

Based on *The Snoopy Show* episode "Nest Friends"
written by Alex Galatis
Adapted by Ximena Hastings
Ready-to-Read

Simon Spotlight
New York   London   Toronto   Sydney   New Delhi

SIMON SPOTLIGHT

An imprint of Simon & Schuster Children's Publishing Division

1230 Avenue of the Americas, New York, New York 10020

This Simon Spotlight edition August 2021

Peanuts and all related titles, logos, and characters are trademarks of

Peanuts Worldwide LLC © 2021 Peanuts Worldwide LLC.

SIMON SPOTLIGHT, READY-TO-READ, and colophon are registered trademarks of

Simon & Schuster, Inc. For information about special discounts for bulk purchases,

please contact Simon & Schuster Special Sales at 1-866-506-1949 or

business@simonandschuster.com.

Manufactured in the United States of America 0721 LAK

10 9 8 7 6 5 4 3 2 1

ISBN 978-1-5344-9439-8 (hc)

ISBN 978-1-5344-9438-1 (pbk)

ISBN 978-1-5344-9440-4 (ebook)

It was a perfect fall day,
and Snoopy was resting
on his doghouse.

Suddenly, a bright orange leaf
landed on his nose.

Then more leaves
landed on him!
Argh! Snoopy thought.

Snoopy knew just what to do.
Ta-da! he thought proudly,
pulling out his leaf blower.

Snoopy blew the leaves away
but noticed one leaf floating
above him.

Snoopy giggled and ran
around the park, trying
to keep the leaf afloat.
But he didn't notice
Lucy and Sally.

"Hey, you just blew away
a nickel's worth of business!"
Lucy shouted.

Then Snoopy blew away
Rerun's sandcastle!

Snoopy chased the leaf
right into Charlie Brown!
He was trying to get
his kite up.

"Wow! I'm actually flying a kite!" Charlie Brown yelled. Then his kite flew right into the Kite-Eating Tree.

Woodstock watched
Snoopy from his
nest and applauded.

Suddenly, he noticed Snoopy
getting closer and closer.
Woodstock held on to his nest,
but it was too late.

Snoopy's leaf blower blew
Woodstock's home away.

Woodstock screamed at
Snoopy, shaking him
back to the present.

Snoopy looked around and
realized this was all his fault.

Snoopy tried to rebuild
Woodstock's home,
with no luck.
Woodstock started sobbing.

Snoopy felt sad
for his best friend.
Then he had an idea. . . .
They could live together!

They imagined all the fun times they could have together.

They could play chess,

dance to music,

and enjoy their favorite root beer!

Snoopy and Woodstock
hugged happily. They would be
best friends . . . and roommates!

Woodstock moved in,
but things didn't go
exactly as they hoped. . . .

Woodstock pulled out his
magazine to read when . . .
BOING!
A dog treat landed on his head.

Later, Snoopy settled down
to paint when . . . *BLAST!*

Woodstock was playing
loud music!
The noise pushed Snoopy's
paintbrush off course.

On another day, Woodstock insisted on watching a TV show Snoopy didn't like.

And he wouldn't give up the remote control!

And then Snoopy tasted
some of Woodstock's birdseed.
Yuck! Snoopy thought,
spitting it all out.

One night, Snoopy was
sleeping when he heard
loud music thumping.

Woodstock was having a party!

Snoopy had had enough.
He pulled his leaf blower
out and began to blow!

Woodstock got his own
mini leaf blower out.
It was a showdown!

After a while, the two friends
looked at the damage.

Snoopy's doghouse was a wreck!
But Woodstock had an idea. . . .

They rebuilt their nest home!
They were still best friends.
And now they were best
nest friends!